In the bewitching embrace of midnight, when the world is cloaked in shadows and the ordinary surrenders to the extraordinary, a realm of spectral mysteries unfolds. Welcome to "Ghosts of Midnight: Haunting Tales After Dark."

Within the pages of this chilling anthology, darkness becomes a canvas for the supernatural, and the veil between the living and the departed grows thin. These tales are not for the faint of heart, as they traverse the eerie landscapes of haunted realms, mysterious apparitions, and otherworldly encounters.

As the clock strikes twelve, prepare to embark on a journey into the unknown, where each story is a portal to a realm where the line between the living and the dead blurs. Here, the ghosts of midnight emerge from the depths of the shadows to share their haunting tales after dark.

Turn the page, if you dare, and step into a world where whispers in the night may be more than just the wind, and the creaking floorboards might be a prelude to something otherworldly. "Ghosts of Midnight: Haunting Tales After Dark" invites you to explore the mysteries that unfold when the moon is high, and the supernatural awakens in the silent hours. Brace yourself for a collection of stories that will linger in your thoughts long after the last echoes of midnight have faded away.

Table of Contents

Page 4 - The Mirror's Reflection
Page 9 - The Cursed Symphony
Page 13 - The Whispering Woods
Page 18 - The Haunting Melody of Ravenscroft Manor
Page 23 - The Shadows of Forgotten Asylum
Page 29 - The Lighthouse Keeper's Lament
Page 35 - The Phantom Masquerade
Page 41 - The Spectral Carnival
Page 48 - The Forgotten Library of Shadows
Page 54 - The Whispering Grove
Page 60 - The Silent Cathedral of Echoes
Page 66 - The Phantom Carnival of Desires
Page 73 - The Veil of Forgotten Souls
Page 79 - The Midnight Masquerade of Eternal Enchantment
Page 85 - The Cryptic Clocktower of Time's Embrace
Page 92 - The Ethereal Lighthouse of Lost Souls
Page 98 - The Whispers in the Enchanted Garden
Page 104 - The Celestial Observatory of Astral Echoes
Page 110 - The Haunted Theater of Spectral Performances
Page 116 - The Cursed Manor of Eternal Whispers
Page 122 - The Enigmatic Resonance of Pensacola's Haunted Theater
Page 131 - The Nightmarish Road to Horror Con
Page 141 - About the Autho

The Mirror's Reflection

As the moon hung low in the velvety sky, casting an ethereal glow upon an ancient mansion, a solitary figure named Emily found herself drawn to an ornate mirror in the grand hallway. The mansion, long abandoned and rumored to be haunted, had become the subject of local legends and ghostly tales.

On this particular night, Emily's curiosity outweighed her apprehension. The mirror, adorned with intricate silver filigree, seemed to beckon her closer. As she gazed into its depths, her reflection stared back, but something was amiss. The eyes in the mirror held a sorrowful depth, a whisper of secrets untold.

Suddenly, the mansion's atmosphere changed. A cold breeze swept through the hallway, extinguishing the candles that lined the walls. Shadows danced on the periphery of Emily's vision, and the air became heavy with an unseen presence.

In the mirror, Emily witnessed a spectral figure materializing behind her. A woman in a flowing, tattered gown, her eyes filled with longing. Emily turned around, but there was no one there. The figure existed only in the haunted reflection.

Compelled by an otherworldly force, Emily felt a connection with the ghostly woman. The mirror became a portal between the living and the dead. The spectral woman extended a translucent hand, and against her better judgment, Emily reached out to touch it.

As their hands met, a surge of memories flooded Emily's mind. The mansion's past unfolded before her eyes—the tragic love story, the betrayal, and the untimely death that had left the woman's spirit trapped within the mirror.

In that moment, Emily became the conduit between two worlds. Determined to free the trapped soul, she embarked on a quest to uncover the truth behind the mansion's haunting. The journey revealed hidden chambers, forgotten letters, and a love that defied time.

As the clock struck midnight, Emily stood before the mirror, holding the key to release the ghostly woman's spirit. A soft whisper echoed through the mansion, expressing gratitude and bidding farewell. The mirror's surface rippled, and the ethereal figure faded away, leaving only the moonlit reflection of a relieved Emily.

The mansion, once haunted by tragedy, now stood silent and still. Emily, forever changed by the encounter, carried the bittersweet tale of the mirror's reflection—a story of love, loss, and the power of a connection that transcended the boundaries between life and death. And so began the haunting tales after dark in "Ghosts of Midnight: Haunting Tales After Dark."

The Cursed Symphony

In the heart of a forgotten town, shrouded in mist and mystery, stood an old opera house, abandoned for decades. Legend had it that the ghostly echoes of a tragic performance lingered within its walls, haunting the souls brave enough to enter. One fateful night, a young musician named Adrian, seeking inspiration for his compositions, decided to explore the decaying theater.

As he stepped through the creaking doors, the air thickened with the residue of sorrow. The dilapidated grandeur of the opera house seemed frozen in time. Adrian ventured into the auditorium, drawn to the stage where a once-majestic piano stood covered in a dusty white sheet.

Driven by a haunting curiosity, he unveiled the piano and began to play. The first notes echoed through the desolate hall, and with each keystroke, a melancholic melody filled the air. Unbeknownst to Adrian, the ghostly audience, long gone but not forgotten, gathered to witness the spectral reawakening of the cursed symphony.

As the music swirled, shadows danced on the walls, and the ethereal audience materialized in their ghostly splendor. Their eyes, filled with an insatiable longing, fixed upon Adrian. The cursed symphony, a tale of unrequited love and betrayal, unfolded through his fingertips.

Caught in the spectral performance, Adrian became a vessel for the unresolved emotions that permeated the opera house. The ghostly figures wept and danced, reliving the tragic tale that had unfolded on that very stage decades ago.

As the final note resonated, a profound silence enveloped the theater. The ghostly audience faded away, leaving Adrian alone in the haunting aftermath. The cursed symphony had reached its conclusion, and the weight of the past lifted from the forsaken opera house.

Haunted by the bittersweet melody, Adrian emerged from the theater, forever changed. The music he had played that night echoed in his soul, a testament to the inexplicable connection between the living and the dead. The old opera house, having shared its spectral secrets, stood silent once more, awaiting the next seeker of inspiration.

And so, the cursed symphony became another tale etched in the haunted annals of "Ghosts of Midnight: Haunting Tales After Dark."

The Whispering Woods

Nestled at the edge of a small village, the Whispering Woods earned its name from the eerie sounds that seemed to emanate from its depths. Locals spoke of an ancient curse and forbade anyone from entering after nightfall. However, curiosity often triumphs over caution.

One moonlit night, a wanderer named Evelyn arrived in the village seeking shelter. Intrigued by the ominous reputation of the Whispering Woods, she decided to spend the night beneath its shadowy canopy. As the village slept, she ventured into the woods, guided only by the soft glow of fireflies.

The air within the Whispering Woods felt charged with an otherworldly energy. Strange murmurs and faint whispers accompanied Evelyn's every step. She soon stumbled upon an ancient tree with gnarled roots and silver bark. Engraved with mysterious symbols, it seemed to beckon her closer.

As Evelyn approached, the whispers intensified, telling tales of long-forgotten enchantments and the spirits that guarded the heart of the woods. Drawn to the mystic energy, she touched the ancient tree, awakening a dormant magic that connected her to the spirits of the Whispering Woods.

Invisible threads wove through the air, creating a spectral path that led Evelyn deeper into the heart of the enchanted forest. Illuminated by the ethereal glow, ghostly figures emerged from the trees, their eyes reflecting centuries of wisdom and longing.

The spirits shared their stories—of love and loss, ancient alliances, and the curse that bound them to the Whispering Woods. Evelyn, now a conduit between the living and the ethereal, listened with rapt attention as the tales unfolded like petals in a haunted bloom.

Determined to break the curse, Evelyn embarked on a quest to uncover the source of the enchantment. The Whispering Woods guided her through hidden clearings and ghostly glades, revealing secrets that intertwined with the very roots of the ancient tree.

As dawn approached, Evelyn stood before the enchanted tree, armed with newfound knowledge. With a whispered incantation, she unraveled the threads of the curse, freeing the spirits that had long been imprisoned. The woods fell silent, and the ancient tree shimmered with gratitude.

Evelyn emerged from the Whispering Woods, carrying the stories of the spirits and the echoes of their gratitude. The village awoke to find the once forbidding woods transformed into a haven of peace. The curse had lifted, and the Whispering Woods whispered tales of gratitude to those who dared to listen.

And so, another spectral saga unfolded within the pages of "Ghosts of Midnight: Haunting Tales After Dark."

The Haunting Melody of Ravenscroft Manor

Ravenscroft Manor stood atop a desolate hill, its silhouette haunting the moonlit landscape. Once a grand estate, it had fallen into disrepair, its walls echoing with the ghostly remnants of a bygone era. The townsfolk spoke of a forbidden melody that played at midnight, a cursed song that bound the spirits within.

A curious musician named Gabriel, drawn by tales of the haunted manor, arrived in the nearby village. Intrigued by the promise of a supernatural symphony, he decided to spend a night within the decaying walls of Ravenscroft Manor.

As the clock struck midnight, Gabriel entered the manor's grand ballroom, where a dilapidated grand piano awaited beneath a tattered chandelier. The air grew heavy with anticipation as he hesitantly placed his fingers on the ivory keys. To his surprise, a haunting melody, long imprisoned, began to emanate from the instrument.

The ballroom came alive with ethereal dancers, their gowns and suits of a bygone era swaying to the spectral melody. Gabriel, entranced by the supernatural waltz, found himself at the center of the ghostly gathering. The spirits, unable to rest, sought solace in the haunting notes that echoed through the manor.

As the music continued, the spirits' stories unfolded. A tragic love affair, betrayal, and a family torn apart by greed—each note carried the weight of untold sorrows. Gabriel became a conduit for the spirits' emotions, channeling their stories through the haunting melody.

The ballroom transformed into a spectral stage, and the spirits performed their tragic tale with ghostly grace. Gabriel, overwhelmed by the intensity of the supernatural symphony, felt the emotions of the spirits coursing through him like an otherworldly current.

Determined to bring closure to the tormented souls, Gabriel delved into the manor's history. Hidden passages revealed family secrets and a cursed legacy that bound the spirits to Ravenscroft Manor. The musician's quest for resolution intertwined with the ghostly narrative, blurring the lines between the living and the dead.

As the first light of dawn approached, Gabriel uncovered a long-lost relic—a locket that held the key to breaking the curse. With a whispered incantation and a heartfelt melody, he set the spirits free. The grand ballroom fell silent, the spectral dancers fading away into the morning mist.

Gabriel emerged from Ravenscroft Manor, forever changed by the haunting melody that had echoed through the night. The once-forbidding estate now stood silent, its cursed legacy lifted. The town, waking to a new day, would remember the musician who had orchestrated the release of the spirits within the haunted halls.

And so, Ravenscroft Manor added its spectral notes to the symphony of tales in "Ghosts of Midnight: Haunting Tales After Dark."

The Shadows of Forgotten Asylum

Amidst the sprawling hills, hidden by overgrown vegetation, lay the remnants of the Forgotten Asylum—an imposing structure with a dark history that cast a long shadow over the land. The asylum, abandoned for decades, held the secrets of tortured souls and the lingering echoes of unspeakable horrors.

A daring journalist named Olivia, driven by a fascination with the macabre, decided to explore the decaying asylum in search of a story that would send shivers down the spines of her readers. Armed with a flashlight and a notebook, she crossed the threshold into the realm of forgotten nightmares.

The air within the asylum was thick with a chilling stillness, broken only by the sound of Olivia's footsteps echoing through the empty halls. As she ventured deeper, she noticed shadows that seemed to move on their own, twisting and contorting as if trying to escape the confines of the decaying walls.

Guided by an unexplained compulsion, Olivia reached the asylum's underground chambers—once the epicenter of unspeakable experiments. The flickering light revealed remnants of restraints and haunting etchings on the walls, each telling a tale of despair and madness.

In one particularly ominous chamber, Olivia discovered a forgotten journal, its pages filled with the scribblings of a tormented soul. The author, a former inmate, spoke of shadows that whispered malevolent secrets, promising release from the asylum's torment. The journalist's curiosity turned to unease as she realized that the shadows around her seemed to respond to the words on the pages.

As midnight approached, the asylum seemed to come alive with ghostly apparitions. Tormented spirits materialized, their hollow eyes fixed on

Olivia. The shadows, now more pronounced, danced with malevolence, whispering fragments of forgotten memories and the anguish of those who had suffered within the asylum's grim embrace.

Determined to unveil the truth, Olivia delved into the journal's cryptic passages. Each revelation led her deeper into the asylum's haunted history—a tale of unethical experiments, lost humanity, and the malevolent force that had claimed the souls within.

The shadows, now a swirling maelstrom of darkness, surrounded Olivia. She felt the weight of the asylum's tragic past pressing upon her, an oppressive force that sought to ensnare her in its spectral grasp. Yet, fueled by a journalist's relentless pursuit of truth, she pressed on.

As the clock struck midnight, Olivia uncovered the asylum's darkest secret—an otherworldly entity that thrived on the suffering of the forgotten souls. Armed with this revelation, she confronted the malevolent force, challenging it with the stories of the tormented spirits.

With a burst of ethereal energy, the shadows retreated, their malevolence dissipating into the cold, night air. The asylum, once a bastion of darkness, now stood silent, its haunted corridors bereft of the spectral shadows that had long tormented it.

Olivia emerged from the Forgotten Asylum, haunted by the stories she had uncovered. The night had revealed not only the chilling secrets of the decaying structure but also the resilience of the human spirit against the forces of darkness. The forgotten asylum, its shadows now dispersed, became another chapter in the haunting tales of "Ghosts of Midnight: Haunting Tales After Dark."

The Lighthouse Keeper's Lament

Perched on a desolate cliff overlooking a tumultuous sea, the Beacon's Embrace Lighthouse stood as a solitary sentinel against the relentless waves. For generations, the lighthouse had guided sailors safely to shore, but behind its weathered exterior lay a tale of love and tragedy that haunted the coastal town.

In the 19th century, a lighthouse keeper named Samuel tended to the beacon with unwavering dedication. His life was solitary, accompanied only by the rhythmic pulse of the waves and the haunting calls of distant seabirds. One stormy night, a shipwreck left a lone survivor—a mysterious woman named Isabella, with sea-soaked clothes and haunted eyes.

Samuel, captivated by Isabella's enigmatic presence, nursed her back to health within the lighthouse's stark confines. As the storm raged outside, the two found solace in each other's company, their connection deepening as they shared tales of their pasts and dreams for the future.

As the tempest subsided, Isabella revealed a tragic secret—she was a ghost, bound to the lighthouse by an unfulfilled promise made in a bygone era. The revelation did little to dampen the growing affection between Samuel and Isabella. Their love defied the boundaries between the living and the dead, creating a sanctuary within the lighthouse's stoic walls.

Nights were filled with whispered promises, and days were spent tending to the lighthouse. The beacon, fueled not only by oil but by the undying love of two souls, shone brighter than ever before. The townsfolk, unaware of the supernatural love story unfolding within the lighthouse, marveled at the luminous glow that guided ships to safety.

As years passed, Samuel and Isabella's bond deepened. Yet, the weight of Isabella's unfulfilled promise cast a looming shadow over their happiness. Desperate to break the curse that bound her, the couple delved into ancient texts and sought the guidance of mystics to unravel the mysteries of Isabella's past.

Midnight became a sacred time within the lighthouse—a moment when the veil between the living and the spectral realms thinned. Samuel and Isabella conducted rituals, hoping to find a way to release her from the ethereal chains that bound her to the Beacon's Embrace.

One fateful midnight, as a spectral mist enveloped the lighthouse, a ethereal figure appeared—a harbinger of Isabella's past. The ghostly messenger revealed the key to breaking the curse—a selfless act of love that transcended time and mortality.

Determined to set Isabella free, Samuel made the ultimate sacrifice. In an act of selflessness, he relinquished his mortal existence, his love for Isabella serving as a beacon of light that pierced through the veil of the supernatural. As Samuel's spirit merged with the sea breeze, Isabella was released from her spectral shackles.

The lighthouse, now bathed in a radiant glow, stood witness to a love that transcended the boundaries of life and death. Isabella, free to journey into the afterlife, bid a tearful farewell to the lighthouse that had been their sanctuary. The Beacon's Embrace, forever changed by the love story that had unfolded within its walls, continued to guide sailors through the treacherous sea.

And so, the Lighthouse Keeper's Lament joined the ethereal chorus of tales in "Ghosts of Midnight: Haunting Tales After Dark."

The Phantom Masquerade

In the heart of a forgotten city, where cobblestone streets whispered of bygone eras, a dilapidated theater stood as a relic of grandeur. The once-majestic venue, known as the Phantom Masquerade, had hosted opulent celebrations and performances that lingered in the memories of those who had witnessed its glory. However, a dark shadow cast by a tragic event had condemned the theater to an eternity of silence and abandonment.

Enter Eleanor, a talented ballerina with a passion for unraveling mysteries. Drawn to the allure of the Phantom Masquerade, she embarked on a quest to revive the forgotten splendor and uncover the truth behind the tragedy that had left the theater in ruins.

Eleanor, armed with determination and a curiosity that bordered on the supernatural, sought access to the long-sealed doors of the Phantom Masquerade. Her every step echoed through the vast emptiness as she wandered through the grand ballroom, once adorned with chandeliers that cast dancing shadows on the faces concealed by ornate masks.

As midnight approached, a phantom melody reverberated through the theater—an ethereal waltz that seemed to beckon Eleanor to join the unseen dancers. Intrigued and compelled by the supernatural serenade, she donned a forgotten mask from the theater's glory days, its weight a tangible link to the past.

Suddenly, the ballroom came alive with spectral figures, their movements graceful yet melancholic. The phantom dancers, trapped between worlds, twirled and swayed in rhythm with the haunting melody. Eleanor, caught in the spectral dance, found herself immersed in a bygone era, a witness to the grandeur that once graced the Phantom Masquerade.

The ghostly figures, faces hidden behind masks frozen in time, conveyed a tale of unrequited love and a masked ball that had ended in tragedy. Eleanor, guided by the phantom dancers, traced the steps of the ill-fated lovers—the phantom of the masquerade and the ballerina whose heart he had captured.

The spectral waltz reached its climax, revealing the heart-wrenching truth. The phantom, a tormented soul seeking redemption, had orchestrated the masquerade to reunite with his lost love. However, a tragic twist of fate had condemned them to dance through eternity in the limbo between the living and the dead.

Determined to break the cycle of sorrow, Eleanor delved into the Phantom

Masquerade's history. Hidden passages and forgotten letters unveiled the lovers' tale—a story of jealousy, betrayal, and a curse that bound them to the grand ballroom.

As the clock struck midnight, Eleanor confronted the phantom and, with a selfless act of compassion, broke the spectral curse that had tormented the lovers for centuries. The phantom, freed from the ethereal chains, shared a final, melancholic dance with his lost love before vanishing into the moonlit shadows.

The Phantom Masquerade, now touched by the bittersweet echoes of a love redeemed, stood as a testament to the power of compassion and the enduring legacy of the grand ballroom. Eleanor emerged from the theater, her heart heavy with the weight of the phantom's tale, yet uplifted by the knowledge that love had triumphed over the haunting shadows.

And so, the Phantom Masquerade unfolded its ghostly tapestry within the pages of "Ghosts of Midnight: Haunting Tales After Dark."

The Spectral Carnival

In the outskirts of a forgotten town, obscured by the mists of time, an abandoned carnival lay in decay—a once-vibrant spectacle that had faded into the realm of phantoms and echoes. The spectral carnival, with its faded banners and rusted rides, held the memories of a bygone era, concealing the mysteries that had transformed it into a ghostly carnival of the night.

Enter Jackson, a seasoned paranormal investigator with an insatiable curiosity for the unknown. Drawn to the eerie legends surrounding the spectral carnival, he arrived on a moonlit night, armed with a collection of arcane artifacts and an open mind. The air within the carnival carried the lingering laughter of children and the faint strains of a melancholic calliope.

As Jackson ventured deeper into the heart of the carnival, the flickering lights cast eerie shadows on the decaying attractions. The Ferris wheel, now motionless and rusted, stood as a towering sentinel to the ghosts of the past. Unearthly whispers seemed to beckon him toward the center of the spectral carnival—the once-vibrant midway now a realm of forgotten dreams.

The clock neared midnight, and the air grew electric with anticipation. Suddenly, the ghostly remnants of the carnival came alive. Faint echoes of laughter and carnival music intertwined with the soft sobs of trapped spirits, creating a haunting symphony that enveloped Jackson in a spectral embrace.

Amidst the ethereal attractions, Jackson discovered a forgotten tent—a portal to a world between the living and the dead. As he stepped through the worn canvas, he found himself transported to the spectral carnival's heyday. Ghostly revelers danced around him, their faces frozen in expressions of joy and innocence.

In the midst of the spectral carnival, Jackson encountered a ghostly ringmaster—the guardian of the trapped souls. The ringmaster, once a charismatic showman, revealed the carnival's tragic history. A fire, ignited by a long-forgotten accident, had claimed the lives of both performers and attendees, leaving their spirits bound to the carnival grounds.

Haunted by the tale, Jackson felt a profound connection to the trapped souls. He embarked on a journey through the ghostly attractions, interacting with the spirits who yearned for release. Each ghost harbored unfinished business—forgotten promises, unfulfilled dreams, and the lingering pain of a life cut short.

Determined to bring closure to the spectral carnival, Jackson delved into the past, seeking clues that would set the trapped souls free. Hidden diaries and faded photographs unveiled the untold stories of the performers and attendees, each revelation unlocking a new layer of the carnival's haunted legacy.

As the clock struck midnight, Jackson stood at the center of the spectral carnival, armed with the collective tales of the trapped spirits. With a heartfelt plea and an offering of understanding, he invited the spirits to embrace release and move on to the afterlife.

The carnival's atmosphere shifted as a soft wind carried the whispers of gratitude from the freed souls. The flickering lights brightened, and the once-faded banners regained their vibrant hues. The spectral carnival, transformed by the release of trapped spirits, became a beacon of peace within the night.

Jackson emerged from the carnival, his heart heavy with the weight of the stories he had uncovered. The spectral carnival, once a realm of melancholy, now stood as a testament to the resilience of the human spirit and the catharsis that could be found in the embrace of release.

And so, the Spectral Carnival added its ghostly chapter to the unfolding tales in "Ghosts of Midnight: Haunting Tales After Dark."

The Forgotten Library of Shadows

Nestled within the heart of a forgotten town, where the cobblestone streets whispered secrets of yesteryears, stood an ancient library veiled in mystery—the Arcane Archives. This repository of forgotten knowledge, adorned with dust-covered tomes and timeworn manuscripts, had long been abandoned, its once-hallowed halls echoing with the whispers of tales untold.

Enter Amelia, an archeologist with an insatiable thirst for uncovering the enigmatic remnants of the past. Drawn to the hallowed silence that surrounded the Arcane Archives, she embarked on a journey to unearth the forgotten secrets that lay dormant within its shadowy corridors.

The library, with its towering shelves and labyrinthine passages, seemed to resist the intrusion of the modern world. As Amelia traversed the dimly lit aisles, she felt the weight of forgotten knowledge pressing upon her—an unseen force that yearned to share its stories with a curious seeker.

As midnight approached, the ancient tomes began to stir with a spectral energy. The forgotten pages rustled as if turning of their own accord, revealing passages that chronicled tales of arcane rituals, lost civilizations, and a secret society that had safeguarded mystical knowledge for centuries.

Amelia, guided by the flickering light of her lantern, delved into the depths of the Arcane Archives. Hidden chambers concealed artifacts of unimaginable power and forbidden texts that whispered secrets only to those brave enough to seek them. The library became a portal to realms beyond the understanding of mortals.

Within the labyrinth of forgotten knowledge, Amelia uncovered the tale of the library's origins—a pact made by ancient scholars to preserve esoteric wisdom that transcended the boundaries of time. However, a shadowy figure, consumed by the desire for forbidden knowledge, had betrayed the pact, leaving the library to succumb to the weight of forgotten secrets.

Determined to restore the balance, Amelia unearthed a key—a mystical artifact that resonated with the arcane energy of the library. The key opened hidden passages and revealed the truths buried within the forgotten tomes. As she explored the library's hidden recesses, spectral apparitions of the betrayed scholars materialized, expressing gratitude for the chance to share their wisdom once more.

As the clock struck midnight, Amelia stood at the heart of the Arcane Archives, surrounded by the shimmering glow of ancient knowledge. With the mystical key, she initiated a ritual that cleansed the library of its lingering shadows, allowing the spirits of the scholars to find eternal rest.

The once-forgotten library, now bathed in an ethereal radiance, became a beacon of enlightenment. The Arcane Archives, once abandoned and shrouded in mystery, stood as a testament to the enduring power of wisdom and the responsibility of those who sought to uncover the truths hidden within the annals of time.

Amelia emerged from the library, carrying not only the knowledge she had sought but also the gratitude of the spectral scholars. The Forgotten Library of Shadows, with its illuminated corridors and restored sanctity, added its enigmatic tales to the unfolding narratives in "Ghosts of Midnight: Haunting Tales After Dark."

The Whispering Grove

Deep within an ancient forest, where sunlight struggled to pierce the dense canopy, lay the Whispering Grove—an enchanted realm that hummed with the secrets of the natural world. The ancient trees, with their twisted branches, stood as silent sentinels, their leaves rustling with whispers that spoke of forgotten alliances and mystical guardianship.

In the heart of this mystical grove, a young botanist named Olivia felt an unexplainable connection to the whispering leaves. Driven by a passion for the unexplored mysteries of the natural world, she entered the grove on a moonlit night, guided by an unseen force that beckoned her deeper into the woodland sanctuary.

As Olivia ventured further, the air became thick with the fragrance of blooming flowers and the subtle scent of magic that permeated the Whispering Grove. Midnight approached, and the moon cast an ethereal glow, revealing a hidden clearing adorned with phosphorescent flowers that pulsed with an otherworldly light.

In the heart of the clearing stood an ancient tree—the Whispering Willow. Its bark held the echoes of centuries, and its roots intertwined with the very essence of the grove. Olivia, captivated by the mystical energy, reached out to touch the sacred tree, unleashing a surge of ancient magic that bound her fate with the enchanted realm.

As the clock neared midnight, the Whispering Grove came alive with ethereal beings—nature spirits, guardians of the grove, and spectral creatures that materialized in the moonlit haze. Olivia found herself surrounded by the spirits of the woodland, each embodying the essence of a different aspect of nature.

The spirits, with their luminous forms, shared tales of ancient alliances between humanity and the natural world. They spoke of a time when humans and spirits coexisted harmoniously, exchanging wisdom and protection. However, as civilizations grew, the bond weakened, and the Whispering Grove fell into obscurity.

Determined to restore the balance, Olivia embarked on a quest to rediscover the forgotten rituals that once united humans and spirits. Guided by the whispers of the ancient tree and aided by the spirits of the grove, she ventured into hidden glades and secret pools, unlocking the mysteries of nature's ancient covenant.

The Whispering Grove revealed its sacred sites, each holding a fragment of the forgotten alliance. Olivia, guided by the spirits, conducted rituals that honored the natural world and forged a renewed connection between humanity and the enchanted realm. As she delved into the ancient rites, the grove responded with a vibrant energy that resonated with the heartbeat of the earth.

At the stroke of midnight, Olivia stood before the Whispering Willow, the culmination of her quest illuminating the grove with a dazzling radiance. The spirits, once ethereal and distant, merged with the natural world, their forms intertwining with the leaves, flowers, and ancient trees.

The Whispering Grove, now reawakened, stood as a sanctuary where the spirits and humans could once again coexist in harmony. Olivia, forever changed by the mystical alliance, emerged from the grove as a guardian of its secrets and a bearer of the whispers that echoed through the ancient trees.

And so, the Whispering Grove added its enchanted verses to the mesmerizing tales within "Ghosts of Midnight: Haunting Tales After Dark."

The Silent Cathedral of Echoes

Nestled within the heart of a forgotten city, shrouded in mist and memories, the Silent Cathedral of Echoes stood as a testament to an age long past. Its towering spires, adorned with intricate carvings, rose like silent sentinels against the moonlit sky. The cathedral, abandoned for centuries, held within its sacred walls the haunting whispers of bygone prayers and untold stories.

Intrigued by the tales of the silent cathedral, a historian named Adrian embarked on a journey to unveil the mysteries that lay dormant within its stone corridors. Guided by ancient manuscripts and weathered maps, he entered the city's desolate center on a night when the air seemed to carry the ethereal echoes of forgotten hymns.

As Adrian crossed the threshold of the cathedral, the heavy wooden doors groaned in protest, revealing a vast sanctuary adorned with faded tapestries and decaying pews. The grandeur of the silent cathedral, once a beacon of divine worship, now stood as a solemn witness to the passage of time.

As midnight approached, the cathedral's silence seemed to intensify, creating an eerie atmosphere that heightened Adrian's senses. Soft whispers echoed through the nave, as if the very stones retained the memories of long-vanished congregations. The historian felt an invisible presence, an ethereal congregation that lingered within the sacred space.

Driven by an inexplicable curiosity, Adrian explored the hidden chambers and forgotten catacombs beneath the cathedral. Secret passages revealed cryptic inscriptions, each telling a tale of ancient rites and spiritual mysteries. The silent cathedral, it seemed, held within its depths the echoes of a clandestine order devoted to the pursuit of divine knowledge.

As Adrian delved deeper into the cathedral's secrets, he uncovered a chamber veiled in darkness—an ancient library that cradled forbidden tomes and illuminated manuscripts. The pages whispered stories of celestial realms, divine visions, and the pursuit of transcendence that had drawn seekers to the silent cathedral throughout the ages.

Guided by the ethereal whispers, Adrian deciphered the sacred texts and rituals that once echoed through the silent cathedral's hallowed halls. The forgotten order, devoted to unlocking the mysteries of the divine, had practiced rites that transcended the boundaries of mortal understanding.

At the stroke of midnight, within the silent cathedral's nave, Adrian conducted a ritual drawn from the ancient texts. The air shimmered with a celestial energy, and the echoes of hymns long silenced reverberated through the sacred space. The invisible congregation, once lost to time, materialized as shimmering apparitions, their faces serene with the knowledge of divine truths.

The silent cathedral, once dormant in its abandonment, now pulsed with a celestial energy that transcended the earthly realm. Adrian, standing amidst the ethereal congregation, felt the weight of centuries of prayers and spiritual quests that had shaped the silent cathedral into a sanctuary of mystic echoes.

As the night embraced the silent cathedral, Adrian emerged from its sacred embrace, forever changed by the unearthed secrets and celestial echoes. The forgotten sanctuary, now rekindled with divine energy, added its mystic resonance to the unfolding tales in "Ghosts of Midnight: Haunting Tales After Dark."

The Phantom Carnival of Desires

In the outskirts of a long-forgotten town, where the echoes of laughter had faded into the rustle of winds through desolate streets, the Phantom Carnival of Desires emerged from the mists of time. Its spectral tents and ethereal attractions beckoned to those who dared to seek the fulfillment of their deepest longings. Legends spoke of a carnival that materialized only on moonlit nights, offering a chance for the living to confront their unspoken desires.

Drawn by the haunting tales surrounding the Phantom Carnival, a wanderer named Elara arrived in the town. Intrigued by the whispers of an otherworldly spectacle, she ventured into the heart of the forsaken streets on a night when the moon cast an enchanting glow upon the spectral tents.

The Phantom Carnival, with its faded banners and ghostly lights, unfolded before Elara like a mirage of forgotten dreams. The air hummed with an electric energy, and the distant sounds of spectral music mingled with the soft murmur of unseen whispers. As she stepped through the entrance, the carnival embraced her with an otherworldly warmth.

Midnight approached, and the Phantom Carnival seemed to awaken with a spectral life of its own. Attractions flickered to life, revealing phantasmal visions that mirrored the desires buried within the hearts of those who sought refuge within the carnival's embrace. Elara, intrigued and cautious, navigated through the ethereal attractions that promised to unveil the depths of her own unspoken longings.

The first attraction, the Mirror Maze of Reflections, revealed hidden facets of Elara's past and the choices that had shaped her journey. Spectral reflections danced within the mirrors, capturing moments of joy and sorrow that had become fragments of her identity. The echoes of laughter and tears intertwined in a haunting symphony.

As Elara ventured deeper, she encountered the Carousel of Whispers—a spectral ride that carried riders through the realms of their innermost desires. The phantom horses galloped in tandem with the unspoken wishes of each rider, their ethereal forms reflecting the untapped aspirations that lingered within Elara's soul.

Guided by the whispers of the carnival, Elara found herself at the heart of the Fortune Teller's Tent—a place where destiny intertwined with desire. The enigmatic fortune teller, cloaked in shadows, unraveled the threads of Elara's future, revealing the untold possibilities that awaited her should she confront her deepest desires.

The climax of the Phantom Carnival unfolded beneath the Ghostly Ferris Wheel—a ride that elevated seekers to the heights of their aspirations. As Elara ascended, she glimpsed visions of her ideal future—a tapestry woven with the threads of dreams, ambitions, and the unexplored realms of the heart.

At the stroke of midnight, Elara stood at the center of the Phantom Carnival, her journey through desires complete. The ethereal attractions faded into the night, leaving her with the echoes of revelations and the lingering warmth of the spectral embrace. The carnival, having served as a conduit for self-discovery, vanished into the mists, awaiting the next seeker.

Elara emerged from the forsaken town, forever changed by the Phantom Carnival's revelations. The whispers of desires, once concealed in the recesses of her being, now echoed in harmony with the night wind—a testament to the transformative power of the ethereal spectacle that had unfolded within the Phantom Carnival of Desires.

And so, the Phantom Carnival added its spectral melodies to the haunting tales within the pages of "Ghosts of Midnight: Haunting Tales After Dark."

The Veil of Forgotten Souls

In a secluded valley, cloaked in perpetual mist and veiled by the shadows of towering peaks, lay the Veil of Forgotten Souls—a mysterious realm where the boundaries between the living and the spectral realms blurred into an ethereal tapestry. The valley, shrouded in an otherworldly silence, held the memories of souls long departed, their echoes entwined with the very fabric of the mystical landscape.

A wanderer named Cyrus, burdened by the weight of his own haunted past, stumbled upon the entrance to the valley during a journey through remote lands. Drawn by an inexplicable force, he crossed the threshold into the Veil of Forgotten Souls on a night when the moon cast an ethereal glow upon the mist-shrouded terrain.

As Cyrus ventured deeper into the valley, the air grew thick with a palpable energy—a tapestry of whispers that danced on the breeze. Midnight approached, and the veil between the realms seemed to thin, allowing the echoes of forgotten souls to manifest in subtle shades of mist and shadow.

The spectral landscape unfolded before Cyrus like an ever-shifting dreamscape. Ancient ruins, overgrown with spectral vines, hinted at the existence of a long-lost civilization whose stories were woven into the very soil of the Veil. Cyrus, guided by the ephemeral echoes, explored the remnants of forgotten settlements and ethereal structures.

Within the spectral glades, Cyrus encountered apparitions of the forgotten—a silent procession of souls that moved with a mournful grace. Each spirit bore the weight of unresolved stories and unfulfilled legacies. As Cyrus approached, the apparitions beckoned him to bear witness to their untold tales.

Guided by the spectral echoes, Cyrus discovered the Whispering Pool—a tranquil reservoir that reflected the memories of the forgotten souls. As he gazed into the waters, the surface shimmered with images of lives once lived—triumphs and tragedies, loves found and lost, all suspended in the haunting embrace of the Veil.

The heart of the valley revealed the Forgotten Temple—an ancient structure adorned with ethereal symbols that pulsed with supernatural energy. Within its hallowed halls, Cyrus unearthed the sacred rites and rituals that bound the spirits to the Veil. A vow unfulfilled, an ancient curse, and the timeless yearning for release emerged as threads woven into the spectral fabric of the valley.

At the stroke of midnight, Cyrus stood at the nexus of the Veil of Forgotten Souls, a conduit between the living and the spectral. Guided by the revelations he had unearthed, he conducted a ritual—a solemn ceremony that acknowledged the pain of the forgotten and sought to mend the tears in the fabric of their existence.

The Veil responded with a symphony of whispers, as the spectral echoes began to dissipate into the night. The mournful procession of forgotten souls transformed into a gentle breeze that carried their stories into the cosmic winds. The ancient ruins, once weighed down by the sorrow of the departed, became enshrouded in a luminescent glow.

Cyrus emerged from the Veil, a witness to the transformative power of acknowledging the forgotten. The valley, once cloaked in a somber silence, now resonated with a serenity that echoed the release of lingering souls. The Veil of Forgotten Souls, forever altered by the ritual of remembrance, added its enigmatic tales to the timeless narratives in "Ghosts of Midnight: Haunting Tales After Dark."

The Midnight Masquerade of Eternal Enchantment

In the heart of a forgotten city, where cobblestone streets whispered of a bygone era, an imposing mansion stood as a silent witness to centuries of secrets. This mansion, veiled in ivy and shrouded in the mysteries of time, became the stage for the Midnight Masquerade of Eternal Enchantment—an otherworldly soirée that transcended the boundaries between the living and the spectral.

Amelia, a curious socialite with an insatiable appetite for the extraordinary, stumbled upon the legends surrounding the Midnight Masquerade. Drawn by the allure of an enchanting gathering that materialized only when the moon reached its zenith, she embarked on a quest to unveil the secrets concealed within the mansion's opulent halls.

As midnight approached, Amelia arrived at the mansion's entrance, where an ethereal glow illuminated the grand staircase. The air tingled with an intoxicating energy, and the rustle of phantom footsteps echoed through the grand foyer. The mansion seemed to come alive, its walls pulsating with a spectral heartbeat that guided Amelia deeper into its enigmatic embrace.

The Midnight Masquerade unfolded in the grand ballroom, adorned with chandeliers that cast a soft, ethereal glow. Spectral figures, elegantly dressed in attire spanning across the ages, twirled and swayed in a dance that defied the constraints of time. The masquerade masks concealed the identities of the attendees, each mask a veil that blurred the lines between the living and the departed.

Guided by the spectral waltz, Amelia joined the dance, her gown swishing in harmony with the haunting melodies that reverberated through the ballroom. The masked figures, seemingly lost in the rhythms of eternity, conveyed tales of love, tragedy, and the unyielding bonds that tethered them to the Midnight Masquerade.

Amelia's masked partner, a phantom draped in the elegance of a bygone era, led her through the spectral dance. With each step, he whispered fragments of his own tale—a tragic romance that had transcended lifetimes, a love that defied the inevitability of death. The dance became a journey through the ages, a testament to the enduring power of love that echoed through the Midnight Masquerade.

In the midst of the spectral revelry, Amelia discovered the Veiled Gallery—a hidden alcove adorned with portraits that seemed to capture the essence of souls suspended in the tapestry of eternity. The eyes of the painted figures followed her every movement, and their silent expressions conveyed stories of joy and heartache, eternally preserved within the canvas.

As midnight's embrace tightened, the grand clock in the ballroom struck twelve, signaling the culmination of the Midnight Masquerade. The spectral figures, their masks concealing enigmatic smiles, gathered at the center of the ballroom. The room bathed in an otherworldly light as the spirits bid farewell to the living, their ephemeral presence leaving a lingering enchantment.

Amelia, standing at the threshold of the grand ballroom, witnessed the spectral figures dissipate into the shadows, their tales interwoven with the echoes of the Midnight Masquerade. The mansion, now shrouded in silence, stood as a testament to the ephemeral magic that unfolded within its walls.

Emerging from the enchanting embrace of the Midnight Masquerade of Eternal Enchantment, Amelia carried with her the indelible memories of a dance that transcended the boundaries of time and mortality. The mansion, forever touched by the spectral waltz, added its chapter to the mesmerizing tales within "Ghosts of Midnight: Haunting Tales After Dark."

The Cryptic Clocktower of Time's Embrace

In a forgotten realm, where echoes of ages past lingered in the air, the Cryptic Clocktower of Time's Embrace stood as a monument to the enigma of temporal mysteries. Its spires pierced the heavens, adorned with ancient symbols that whispered tales of epochs long gone. Within its cavernous chambers, the very essence of time seemed to warp and weave through the fabric of reality.

An inquisitive scholar named Evelyn, known for her fascination with arcane knowledge, stumbled upon cryptic manuscripts hinting at the existence of the elusive clocktower. Driven by an insatiable curiosity, she embarked on a perilous journey through uncharted lands, guided by the distant chimes that echoed across the ages.

As Evelyn approached the clocktower's hidden location, the air itself seemed to reverberate with temporal energy. The architecture, an intricate blend of forgotten aesthetics and celestial symbols, stood as a testament to the tower's timeless significance. The entrance revealed a winding staircase that ascended into the heart of the cryptic structure.

At midnight, as Evelyn climbed the spiraling stairs, the chimes of the Cryptic Clocktower resonated with an otherworldly melody. Each toll echoed through the vast expanse, a cosmic chorus that hinted at the tower's profound connection to the mysteries of time. The very walls seemed to ripple with temporal energies as Evelyn reached the tower's zenith.

In the tower's central chamber, a colossal clock, adorned with celestial constellations, dominated the space. The hands of the clock moved with an ethereal grace, marking the passage of moments that transcended the conventional flow of time. Evelyn felt the palpable embrace of temporal forces, as if the very fabric of reality yielded to the influence of the Cryptic Clocktower.

Guided by the cosmic energies, Evelyn uncovered the tower's purpose—a nexus where temporal anomalies converged, allowing glimpses into the past, present, and future. The celestial clock served as a conduit through which individuals could navigate the corridors of time, albeit with great caution and respect for the delicate balance of temporal forces.

Emboldened by her scholarly pursuits, Evelyn activated the arcane machinery within the Cryptic Clocktower, unleashing a cascade of temporal energies that surrounded her in a cosmic dance. Visions of bygone eras manifested in ephemeral wisps, and whispers of the future resonated within the chamber. Evelyn became a temporal voyager, traversing the corridors of time with the Cryptic Clocktower as her celestial guide.

The first glimpse transported Evelyn to an ancient kingdom, where she witnessed the rise and fall of dynasties. The second glimpse immersed her in a futuristic cityscape, revealing technological marvels yet to be realized. Each temporal journey unfolded like chapters in a cosmic tome, a testament to the profound interplay between the Cryptic Clocktower and the fabric of existence.

As midnight's embrace tightened, Evelyn stood at the heart of the Cryptic Clocktower, her temporal voyages etched into the very stones of the chamber. The celestial clock, having revealed the tapestry of time's embrace, chimed a final resonance that echoed through the ages. The tower, forever marked by Evelyn's exploration, stood as a nexus between the known and the unknown.

Exiting the Cryptic Clocktower, Evelyn carried with her the wisdom of temporal mysteries, forever changed by the cosmic dance she had experienced. The tower, now infused with the echoes of her journey, added its enigmatic chapters to the unfolding tales within

"Ghosts of Midnight: Haunting Tales After Dark."

The Ethereal Lighthouse of Lost Souls

Perched upon a desolate cliff, where the turbulent sea met jagged rocks in a symphony of crashing waves, stood the Ethereal Lighthouse of Lost Souls—a beacon that transcended the realms of the mundane. Its weathered exterior bore the scars of countless storms, while its towering spire reached towards the heavens, adorned with a spectral light that beckoned to both the living and the departed.

Marina, a seasoned sailor with tales etched into the lines of her weathered face, had heard whispers of the ethereal lighthouse during her seafaring adventures. Drawn by a mysterious force that tugged at the core of her maritime soul, she set sail on a moonlit night, navigating treacherous waters to reach the remote cliffside where the lighthouse stood sentinel.

As Marina approached the cliff, the air resonated with haunting melodies that seemed to emanate from the lighthouse itself. Midnight's embrace descended upon the sea, shrouding the ethereal structure in an otherworldly glow. The beam of light, refracted through the mist, painted an ephemeral path that danced upon the restless waves.

Entering the lighthouse, Marina discovered an interior bathed in an ambient radiance. The walls were adorned with maritime relics and paintings that told tales of lost ships and sailors claimed by the sea. The ethereal light, emanating from a mystical source at the heart of the spire, pulsed in rhythm with the ebb and flow of the ocean below.

Guided by the spectral glow, Marina ascended the winding staircase that led to the pinnacle of the lighthouse. As she reached the summit, she found herself in a celestial chamber where the boundaries between the mortal and spirit realms blurred. Transparent figures of sailors, their souls forever bound to the sea, gathered in a spectral congregation.

At the center of the chamber, Marina discovered the Celestial Compass—an ancient artifact that resonated with the energies of the ethereal lighthouse. The compass, adorned with symbols of maritime lore, held the power to guide lost souls to their final resting place. Marina, realizing the sacred responsibility bestowed upon her, embraced her role as a custodian of the Celestial Compass.

As the clock struck midnight, the ethereal light intensified, casting a luminous glow that extended far into the horizon. The sea, once turbulent, transformed into a tranquil expanse. Lost souls, drawn by the celestial beacon, materialized as ethereal apparitions, their faces reflecting the gratitude of spirits finding solace.

Guided by the Celestial Compass, Marina embarked on a voyage across the spectral sea, steering an otherworldly vessel that sailed the currents between realms. Each lost soul she encountered shared tales of unfinished voyages, unspoken farewells, and the longing for the embrace of eternal waters.

At the culmination of her ethereal odyssey, Marina stood at the prow of her spectral vessel, surrounded by the liberated souls she had guided. The ethereal lighthouse, now a beacon of tranquility, cast its light upon the departed spirits as they sailed into the cosmic sea, disappearing beyond the veil of the horizon.

Marina, having fulfilled her sacred duty, descended from the ethereal lighthouse with the Celestial Compass in hand. The rhythmic sounds of the sea echoed with a newfound serenity. The lighthouse, forever a conduit between the mortal and spirit realms, added its ethereal verses to the mesmerizing tales within "Ghosts of Midnight: Haunting Tales After Dark."

The Whispers in the Enchanted Garden

Nestled within a forgotten kingdom, where the ivy-clad walls of a crumbling castle stood as relics of forgotten splendor, lay the Enchanted Garden—a realm where magic and nature coalesced in a dance of perpetual twilight. This mystical haven, hidden from the eyes of mortals, held secrets whispered by ancient trees, blooming flowers, and the soft rustle of unseen creatures.

Isabella, a young artist with an affinity for the mystical, uncovered cryptic scrolls that hinted at the existence of the Enchanted Garden. Drawn by the allure of untold wonders, she embarked on a moonlit journey, guided by the ethereal glow that emanated from the heart of the overgrown castle ruins.

As Isabella passed through the remnants of a forgotten archway, the air shimmered with a magical aura. The Enchanted Garden unfolded before her, a dreamscape bathed in hues of moonlight and luminescent flora. Midnight approached, and the garden seemed to awaken with a symphony of whispers that caressed Isabella's senses.

The ancient trees, with branches entwined like guardian spirits, leaned in to share their tales of a time when the kingdom flourished with magic. The blooms, with petals that radiated an ethereal glow, swayed in a dance choreographed by the unseen whims of nature. Isabella, immersed in the enchanting ambiance, felt the garden's pulse resonate with the heartbeat of the earth.

Guided by the soft whispers, Isabella discovered the Fountain of Dreams—a crystalline pool surrounded by iridescent flowers that mirrored the reflections of unfulfilled wishes. As she gazed into the waters, visions of bygone eras and forgotten aspirations materialized, creating a kaleidoscope of dreams that transcended the boundaries of time.

Venturing deeper into the Enchanted Garden, Isabella encountered the Grove of Echoing Memories. Each petal, leaf, and stone seemed to retain imprints of ancient conversations and shared laughter. The whispers of love, betrayal, and friendships long past lingered like a lingering breeze, inviting Isabella to become a silent observer of the garden's timeless tales.

In the heart of the garden, Isabella discovered the Arboreal Throne—an ancient seat carved from the living wood of the oldest tree. As she sat upon the throne, the whispers coalesced into a collective melody—a haunting symphony that narrated the garden's journey through ages of prosperity, decline, and the enduring resilience of nature's magic.

At the stroke of midnight, Isabella stood at the center of the Enchanted Garden, surrounded by the ephemeral glow of mystical flora. The whispers crescendoed into a harmonious chorus, revealing the garden's secret purpose—to be a sanctuary where nature and magic intertwined, perpetuating the cycle of life, decay, and rebirth.

As Isabella left the Enchanted Garden, the echoes of the whispers lingered, etched into her consciousness like a painted canvas of memories. The garden, forever entwined with the essence of her journey, added its enchanting verses to the unfolding tales within "Ghosts of Midnight: Haunting Tales After Dark."

The Celestial Observatory of Astral Echoes

Perched atop a remote mountain, where the veil between the earthly realm and the cosmos grew thin, stood the Celestial Observatory of Astral Echoes—a sanctuary where astronomers and mystics converged to decipher the celestial language written across the night sky. Its towering spires reached towards the cosmos, adorned with ancient runes that held the secrets of astral energies.

A scholar named Elias, known for his fascination with the stars and the esoteric, stumbled upon ancient manuscripts that spoke of the Celestial Observatory. Driven by a cosmic curiosity that transcended the boundaries of mortal understanding, he embarked on a pilgrimage to reach the mountain's summit, guided by the ethereal glow that pulsed from the observatory.

As Elias ascended the mountain, the air became charged with astral energies, and the constellations above seemed to align in a celestial dance. Midnight approached, and the observatory's spires gleamed with an otherworldly luminescence. Elias arrived at the threshold, where the celestial gates awaited to reveal the mysteries that lay beyond.

Entering the observatory, Elias found himself in a celestial chamber adorned with crystalline lenses that refracted the starlight into mesmerizing patterns. Astral charts and celestial maps adorned the walls, depicting the cosmic ballet that unfolded in the vast expanse above. The ethereal hum of celestial energies surrounded Elias as he delved into the observatory's arcane archives.

Guided by the astral echoes, Elias uncovered the Oculus of Stellar Insight—a mystical telescope crafted from meteoric crystal that allowed communion with the celestial realms. As he peered through the oculus, the night sky transformed into a cosmic tapestry, revealing constellations that held the stories of ancient civilizations and the fates of celestial beings.

Venturing to the observatory's zenith, Elias encountered the Astral Oracle—a seer whose eyes reflected the cosmos itself. The oracle spoke in cryptic verses, unraveling the astral destinies that intertwined with the mortal realm. Elias listened as the oracle wove tales of cosmic battles, astral entities that traversed the cosmic currents, and the threads of destiny that bound the stars to the lives below.

In the astral embrace of midnight, Elias engaged in a celestial meditation, allowing his consciousness to soar among the constellations. He communed with astral entities, entities that revealed cosmic truths and the interconnectedness of all existence. The celestial energies resonated with his being, leaving an indelible mark on his mortal soul.

As the clock struck midnight, Elias stood at the pinnacle of the Celestial Observatory of Astral Echoes, surrounded by the shimmering glow of cosmic energies. The observatory, a conduit between the earthly and astral realms, pulsed with the harmonies of the celestial choir. Elias descended from the summit, forever changed by the astral revelations etched into his consciousness.

Exiting the observatory, Elias carried with him the celestial wisdom and the echoes of astral realms. The mountain, crowned by the Celestial Observatory, added its cosmic verses to the enchanting tales within "Ghosts of Midnight: Haunting Tales After Dark."

The Haunted Theater of Spectral Performances

In the heart of an age-old city, where cobblestone streets bore the weight of centuries and the echoes of bygone applause lingered in the air, stood the Haunted Theater of Spectral Performances. Its grand marquee, adorned with ornate letters that spelled tales of enigmatic performances, concealed an otherworldly stage where ethereal actors and phantasmal musicians brought ghostly tales to life.

Victoria, a playwright with an insatiable appetite for the mysterious, uncovered dusty manuscripts that spoke of the

Haunted Theater. Intrigued by the promise of performances that transcended the boundaries between the living and the spectral, she entered the city on a night when the moon cast an enchanting glow upon the forgotten theater.

As Victoria crossed the threshold of the Haunted Theater, the air hummed with a melodic resonance that seemed to emanate from the very walls. Midnight approached, and the ghostly audience, invisible but attentive, filled the ornate seats with anticipatory energy. The stage, illuminated by a spectral spotlight, awaited the unfolding of tales that bridged the realms of the mundane and the ethereal.

The first act, a spectral play titled "The Phantom Masquerade," unfolded with ghostly performers gliding across the stage. Victoria, seated in the shadows, observed as the actors embodied characters from a bygone era—a narrative that transcended the constraints of time. The haunting melodies of a phantom orchestra accompanied the ethereal spectacle, leaving an indelible mark on the audience's spectral senses.

Driven by a desire to understand the mysteries of the Haunted Theater, Victoria delved into the backstage realms where apparitions of stagehands and costume designers worked tirelessly. The ethereal artists, bound by a passion that transcended mortality, crafted sets and costumes that mirrored the grandeur of their performances in life.

Guided by the whispers of the theater's ghostly inhabitants, Victoria discovered the Forgotten Scriptorium—a hidden chamber where the manuscripts of spectral plays were penned by unseen hands. The scripts, inscribed with words that resonated with the echoes of the afterlife, held tales of love, tragedy, and the unfinished stories of those who once graced the Haunted Theater's stage.

The climax of the night unfolded with "The Symphony of Shadows," a spectral musical that merged haunting melodies with ethereal choreography. The conductor, a wraith with a conductor's baton that shimmered with astral energies, directed the phantom musicians who played instruments crafted from moonlight and dreams. The music, a spectral composition that transcended earthly notes, resonated with the emotions of both the living and the departed.

As midnight's embrace tightened, Victoria stood on the stage of the Haunted Theater, surrounded by the echoes of spectral applause. The performers took their bows, their forms merging with the shadows that adorned the stage. The theater, having hosted another spectral performance, seemed to exhale a contented sigh as the ethereal audience dissipated into the night.

Victoria left the Haunted Theater, forever touched by the spectral artistry that unfolded within its hallowed halls. The city, cradling the mysterious stage within its historical embrace, added the haunting verses of the theater's spectral performances to the enchanting tales within "Ghosts of Midnight: Haunting Tales After Dark."

The Cursed Manor of Eternal Whispers

Deep within the heart of a forgotten forest, where ancient trees whispered tales of ages long past, stood the Cursed Manor of Eternal Whispers—a mansion veiled in shadows and bound by a spectral enchantment. Its looming silhouette bore witness to a history steeped in tragedy, its timeworn façade concealing secrets that echoed through the corridors in haunting murmurs.

A historian named Gabriel, fueled by a relentless curiosity for the arcane, stumbled upon cryptic manuscripts that spoke of the Cursed Manor. Drawn to the allure of a dwelling where time seemed to dance with the unseen, he ventured into the heart of the mystical forest on a moonlit night when the boundaries between realms grew thin.

As Gabriel approached the wrought-iron gates of the manor, the air crackled with an ethereal energy. Midnight descended, and the whispers of the forest merged with the haunting murmurs that emanated from the Cursed Manor. The grand entrance, adorned with ivy and ancient runes, creaked open as if inviting him into the realm of eternal whispers.

Within the manor's shadowy halls, Gabriel encountered portraits that seemed to gaze into his very soul. Eyes from centuries past followed his every step, each painted figure telling a tale of lives touched by the enigmatic curse that bound the manor in its spectral embrace. The echoes of laughter, anguish, and forgotten lullabies lingered in the air.

Guided by the ghostly whispers, Gabriel explored hidden chambers and secret passageways that led to forgotten rooms steeped in the mists of time. He uncovered the Grand Library of Lost Chronicles, a repository of arcane tomes that chronicled the manor's cursed legacy—a tale of forbidden pacts, tragic love, and the relentless passage of time.

In the manor's opulent ballroom, Gabriel witnessed apparitions twirling in a spectral dance, frozen in a timeless waltz that echoed the melancholy of forgotten celebrations. The haunting melodies of a ghostly orchestra accompanied the ethereal dance, their instruments playing notes that transcended the boundaries of the mortal realm.

Venturing into the depths of the Cursed Manor, Gabriel discovered the Chamber of Whispers—a sacred space where the curse's origin was said to be intertwined with an ancient artifact known as the Echoing Amulet. As he held the amulet, the whispers intensified, revealing fragments of the manor's tragic history and the yearning souls trapped within its spectral walls.

At the stroke of midnight, Gabriel stood in the heart of the Cursed Manor, the echoes of centuries converging into a haunting symphony. The amulet resonated with an ethereal energy, and the very fabric of the curse seemed to shiver. With a whispered incantation, Gabriel sought to unravel the threads of the curse, releasing the lingering spirits into the cosmic winds.

As the last echoes of the curse dissipated, the Cursed Manor exhaled a sigh of relief, and the air seemed to shimmer with newfound clarity. Gabriel, forever marked by the tales of the haunted dwelling, emerged from the mystical forest carrying the echoes of the manor's eternal whispers. The forest, cradling the Cursed Manor within its ancient embrace, added its spectral verses to the enchanting tales within "Ghosts of Midnight: Haunting Tales After Dark."

The Enigmatic Resonance of Pensacola's Haunted Theater

In the coastal city of Pensacola, where the salty breeze whispered tales of maritime legends, a haunted theater stood as a portal between the worlds of entertainment and the supernatural. The venue, known for hosting concerts that echoed with spectral melodies, had gained a reputation for stirring the spirits that lingered within its historic walls.

Mark and Alan, longtime friends bound by a shared love for music and the unexplained, decided to embark on a journey to Pensacola to attend an Alter

Bridge concert at the renowned Haunted Theater of Resonance. The tales of spectral encounters during live performances added an extra layer of intrigue to their pilgrimage.

As the duo approached the theater on the eve of the concert, the atmosphere buzzed with a palpable energy. Midnight drew near, casting an ethereal glow upon the venue. The marquee, adorned with the names of bands that had graced its stage through the ages, flickered with an otherworldly luminescence that hinted at the enigmatic resonance within.

Upon entering the theater, Mark and Alan felt an immediate shift in the air—a sensation that transcended the anticipation of a live performance. The grand auditorium, with its vintage architecture and plush red seats, exuded a timeless charm that seemed to echo with the cheers and applause of long-gone audiences.

The concert began with Alter Bridge taking the stage, their music resonating through the haunted theater with a potency that reached beyond the realm of the living. The audience, a blend of corporeal and spectral entities, swayed to the melodies, creating a surreal tableau where the boundaries between the mundane and the supernatural blurred.

As Mark and Alan immersed themselves in the music, they noticed flickering lights and shadowy figures that moved in harmony with the haunting rhythms. The spectral audience, seemingly drawn from different eras, stood as silent witnesses to the musical journey unfolding on the stage. Whispers of conversations and fragments of ghostly laughter added an eerie undertone to the ethereal concert experience.

Midway through the performance, an unexpected chill filled the air. The theater's temperature dropped, and the once-flickering lights intensified into a ghostly radiance. Mark and Alan, now acutely aware of the spectral presence around them, felt a subtle touch of unseen hands and heard murmurs that seemed to convey both joy and sorrow.

During a particularly soul-stirring ballad, the theater's grand chandelier began to sway, casting shifting shadows that danced across the ceiling. The ethereal symphony of the Alter Bridge concert merged with the ghostly whispers, creating an atmosphere charged with both musical brilliance and supernatural mystique.

Suddenly, as if a rift between the realms had opened, the specters in the audience began to surge forward, their spectral forms taking on an unsettling intensity. Mark and Alan, initially captivated by the supernatural display, now found themselves in a chilling predicament as the ghostly figures approached with ethereal urgency.

Panicked, the duo tried to retreat from the auditorium, only to find the exit obscured by an otherworldly mist. The once-hospitable theater now felt like a labyrinth of spectral echoes and shifting realities. The ghostly figures, driven by an otherworldly force, closed in on Mark and Alan, their eyes gleaming with an otherworldly intensity.

Desperation gripped Mark and Alan as they navigated the twisting corridors of the haunted theater, pursued by the relentless phantoms. The ethereal melodies that had once enchanted them now seemed to warp into dissonant notes that heightened the sense of impending doom.

In their attempt to escape, the duo stumbled upon hidden passages that seemed to defy the logic of the physical world. The walls whispered cryptic incantations, and doors opened into surreal dimensions where gravity itself seemed to waver. Reality itself became a shifting canvas, and Mark and Alan struggled to maintain their sanity in the face of the spectral onslaught.

As the spectral horde closed in, Mark and Alan discovered a forgotten door that led to the backstage area. The ethereal chorus of the concert now transformed into a dissonant cacophony, the haunting echoes vibrating through the very foundations of the haunted theater. With a burst of adrenaline-fueled determination, the duo rushed through the backstage corridors, pursued by the ghostly legion.

Miraculously finding a concealed exit, Mark and Alan burst into the cool night air of Pensacola, gasping for breath. The haunted theater, now eerily silent, stood in the moonlit night, its enigmatic resonance still echoing through the city. The duo, shaken but alive, exchanged a glance of relief, their hearts pounding from the harrowing encounter with the spectral unknown.

As they left the vicinity of the haunted theater, the eerie mist dissipated, and the spectral echoes faded into the night. The city of Pensacola, cradling the historic venue within its maritime embrace, added the thrilling verses of Mark and Alan's near escape to the enchanting tales within "Ghosts of Midnight: Haunting Tales After Dark."

The Nightmarish Road to Horror Con

Alan and Frank, avid horror enthusiasts, embarked on a road trip to Indianapolis with excitement bubbling in their veins. The anticipation of the horror convention fueled their journey, as they envisioned meeting their favorite actors, collecting rare memorabilia, and reveling in the macabre camaraderie that such events promised.

The road stretched before them, the hum of the engine and the endless expanse of asphalt setting the stage for what would become a nightmarish odyssey. As they approached

Indianapolis, the once-familiar landmarks seemed to take on an eerie aura, casting shadows that whispered foreboding tales.

Upon reaching the convention center, the atmosphere was electric with the buzz of horror aficionados. The air was thick with excitement and anticipation. Little did Alan and Frank know that the convention they had eagerly awaited would turn into a chilling ordeal.

The convention halls were a labyrinth of horror-themed wonders — life-sized monsters, autograph booths, and chilling exhibits. However, a subtle unease lingered beneath the surface. Attendees spoke in hushed tones about strange occurrences — people disappearing and unsettling rumors of ominous figures lurking in the shadows.

Alan and Frank, initially dismissive of the whispers, immersed themselves in the convention's macabre delights. They attended panels, met horror icons, and browsed the vendor booths that showcased everything from vintage memorabilia to cursed artifacts. Yet, a creeping sense of dread lingered, casting a pall over the once-thrilling atmosphere.

As night descended, the convention transformed into a labyrinth of dimly lit corridors and mysterious alcoves. Attendees vanished without a trace, leaving behind only whispers of their disappearance. The air became thick with tension, and the once-vibrant energy now felt suffocating.

In a moment of chilling realization, Alan and Frank found themselves in an isolated section of the convention center. The distant echoes of their footsteps reverberated through eerily quiet corridors. Shadows danced on the walls, seemingly alive with a malevolent intent.

The duo stumbled upon a secluded room where an unsettling tableau awaited them. Life-sized mannequins adorned in horror costumes posed eerily, their glassy eyes seemingly watching the intruders. An ominous silence hung in the air, broken only by the distant sounds of muffled whispers.

Suddenly, a blood-curdling scream shattered the silence. Panic set in as Alan and Frank, now aware of the peril surrounding them, frantically searched for an exit. The convention, once a haven for horror enthusiasts, had transformed into a nightmarish realm where the lines between fiction and reality blurred.

As they navigated the labyrinthine halls, they discovered ominous symbols etched on the walls — arcane markings that hinted at a malevolent force at play. The convention had become a sinister stage where attendees were pawns in a dark, mysterious game.

In their desperate flight, Frank suggested seeking refuge in a nearby bar to regroup and assess the unfolding chaos. Little did they know that the bar, dimly lit and adorned with grotesque decor, would become the setting for the ultimate horror.

As Alan and Frank entered the bar, the atmosphere grew even more unsettling. The patrons, seemingly unaffected by the chaos outside, cast furtive glances in their direction. Unease tightened Alan's chest as he realized the bar was a haven for the mysterious figures orchestrating the nightmarish events.

Frank, seemingly oblivious to the ominous undertones, struck up a conversation with two enigmatic women at the bar. Their alluring smiles masked a sinister intent that sent shivers down Alan's spine. As Frank, fueled by a potent mixture of bravado and naivety, accompanied the women to a secluded corner, the air became charged with an impending malevolence.

In the dimly lit corner, obscured by shadows, Alan watched in horror as the atmosphere shifted. The women's eyes glowed with an unnatural intensity, and the bar's macabre decor seemed to come alive. The patrons, once indifferent, now reveled in a sinister dance that mirrored the unfolding tragedy.

Frank, lost in the allure of the moment, was oblivious to the impending doom. The women, revealing their true vampiric nature, attacked with swift and lethal precision. Alan, paralyzed by fear, could only watch as his friend became ensnared in a deadly embrace.

The bar's atmosphere grew chaotic as the patrons reveled in the gruesome spectacle. Frank's lifeblood drained away, his expression frozen in a mask of terror. The vampires, intoxicated by the macabre ecstasy, reveled in the grisly tableau they had orchestrated.

As the chaos unfolded, Alan summoned the strength to break free from the paralyzing fear. He sprinted through the labyrinthine corridors, his footsteps echoing the heartbeat of a man on the brink of madness. The convention center, now a nightmarish realm, seemed to conspire against his escape.

Miraculously finding an exit, Alan burst into the cool night air of Indianapolis. His breaths came in ragged gasps, and the echoes of the nightmarish events lingered in his mind. The convention center, shrouded in an unsettling silence, stood as a haunting testament to the horrors that had unfolded within.

As Alan left the haunted convention center behind, he carried with him the trauma of that fateful night. The horrors of the horror convention, where reality and the supernatural collided, were etched into his consciousness. The city of Indianapolis, now tainted by the malevolent force that had claimed his friend, added its ominous verses to the haunting tales within "Ghosts of Midnight: Haunting Tales After Dark."

About the Author

Alan Bohms is a distinguished and award-winning figure in the realm of horror cinema, showcasing his versatile talents as an actor, director, and producer. Renowned for his exceptional contributions to the genre, Bohms has left an indelible mark with a string of acclaimed films. Notable works in his repertoire include the chilling "Bermuda Island," the holiday-themed terror of "Mistletoe Massacre," the haunting "Devil's Knight," the extraterrestrial suspense of "Alien Storm," and the enigmatic thriller "Come Here." With a penchant for weaving narratives that send shivers down the audience's spines, Alan Bohms stands as a formidable force in the world of horror entertainment. His award-winning prowess continues to captivate and terrify audiences, solidifying his status as a maestro of the macabre on both sides of the camera.

Made in the USA
Columbia, SC
12 February 2024

fb33563f-11e1-4985-bbe4-41c189db26e6R01